Contents

WHAT'S THE BIG IDEA?

Have you ever looked up at the sky on a really clear, dark night? If so, then you have looked into outer space. Do you believe that life exists out there?

Do you think alien
creatures on some planet
far, far away are looking
up at their night sky
and wondering
'Are we alone?'

5

Our home – planet Earth –
is just a tiny part of the
Universe. A bit like a speck
of dust floating in the
biggest room you can
imagine. The Earth orbits
a star – the Sun.

There are countless stars in the Universe, many of which probably have planets in orbit around them. With all these stars and so much space, can ours really be the only planet to have life?

If life does exist elsewhere in the Universe, why have we found no definite evidence of it yet?

Some people believe that alien creatures have already visited planet Earth in 'flying saucers'. Can they be right?

Many people have seen strange lights in the sky that they believe were alien spacecraft. Some of these sightings have been explained as planets, shooting stars or other natural phenomena. Some are aeroplanes or satellites. Some are hoaxes. However, many are still unexplained. Could they really have been extraterrestrial craft?

If alien life really does exist, will we ever find it? Where and how should we look? Maybe aliens will find us first. Perhaps they have already arrived, but we haven't noticed them because each one is the size of a grain of rice. Would aliens be friendly? Would we be able to communicate with them? What would they look like?

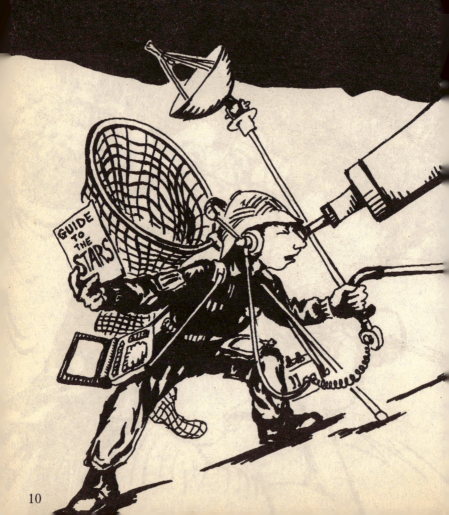

Read on to find some answers to these questions . . .

THE STORY SO FAR...
OR
THE HISTORY OF THE BIG IDEA OF ALIEN LIFE

Who was the first person to wonder whether alien
life exists? We shall never know, but we do know
that the idea is at least about 2,000 years old.
In 70 AD, the Greek writer Plutarch suggested
that there might be demon-like creatures living
on the Moon.

Ideas like Plutarch's were not common at the time, however, because people thought that the Earth, and the creatures on it, held a special place in the Universe . . . right at at the centre.

Until you realise that the Earth is just an ordinary planet orbiting an ordinary star, you can't really open your mind to the possibility of alien life.

● DID YOU KNOW THAT THE OFFICIAL TERM FOR CREATURES LIVING ON THE MOON IS **SELENITES**, AND ON MARS IT IS **MARTIANS**?

A SELENITE

A MARTIAN

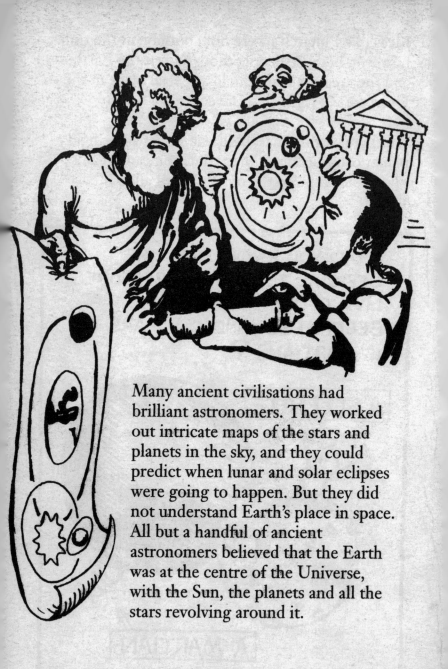

Many ancient civilisations had
brilliant astronomers. They worked
out intricate maps of the stars and
planets in the sky, and they could
predict when lunar and solar eclipses
were going to happen. But they did
not understand Earth's place in space.
All but a handful of ancient
astronomers believed that the Earth
was at the centre of the Universe,
with the Sun, the planets and all the
stars revolving around it.

Almost 1,500 years after Plutarch dreamed up his selenitic demons, the Danish astronomer Nicolaus Copernicus (1473-1543) suggested that the Sun, not the Earth, was at the centre of the Universe. This was wrong, but he did get one important point right: he realised that the Earth and other planets travelled round the Sun. This was an amazing new idea which people found hard to believe at the time. But Copernicus was proved right after his death, thanks to the newly-invented telescope and the clever new maths of the 17th century.

EARTH

THE SUN

OUR SOLAR SYSTEM

Gradually, astronomers realised that the Sun is just an ordinary star, like those points of light in the night sky. The stars of the night sky look much dimmer and smaller than the Sun simply because they are so much further away. The telescope made visible many more stars than the 6,000 or so that can be seen with the naked eye. And there was a bigger surprise to come.

OUR GALAXY

THE SUN

Until the 1920s, it was thought that the Universe went as far as the most distant stars in the night sky. In addition to stars, astronomers had also observed fuzzy patches of light, which they called nebulae.

In 1924, American astronomer Edwin Hubble discovered that some of these nebulae are actually extremely distant and huge groups of stars, much further away than any of the stars in the night sky. Hubble concluded that all the individual stars in our night sky belong to just one galaxy, called the Milky Way, and that there are millions of other galaxies.

In the eyes of astronomers, the Universe had suddenly got much much bigger.

THE HUBBLE TELESCOPE

As astronomers began to discover the true nature of space – including the fact that there may be other planets around other stars – ideas about life elsewhere became more common.

Like Plutarch, the astronomer William Herschel (1738-1822) believed that creatures live on the Moon and on the Sun. Herschel's son John claimed to have seen many weird and wonderful life forms on the Moon through his telescope.

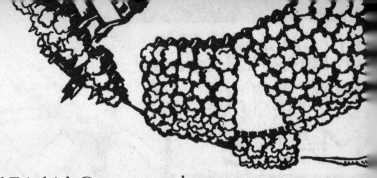

Karl Friedrich Gauss assumed
that there was intelligent life on
other planets in our Solar System.
In 1815, he suggested planting trees in huge
formations, such as right-angled triangles. He
hoped that these would be seen by creatures on
other planets through their telescopes, and that
the aliens would realise that intelligent life
existed here on Earth.

In 1918, Swedish chemist Svante Arrhenius put
forward the idea that life exists everywhere in
the Universe, and is spread from star to star by
tiny spores. Like seeds, these spores
may grow into life as we
know it when they hit a
newly-formed planet.

SCHIAPARELLI'S DRAWING OF MARS

Towards the end of the 19th century, the planet Mars captured the imagination of astronomers and the public. Mars was thought to be the planet most likely to support life, as it is the most similar to Earth.

The public interest in Martians began in 1877, when Italian astronomer Giovanni Schiaparelli made sketches of Mars as he saw it through his telescope. He saw dark lines that he called channels, the Italian word for which is *canali*. American astronomer Percival Lowell heard of Schiaparelli's observations, and was convinced that *canali* meant 'canals'.

Lowell reasoned that Martians had built the canals to irrigate the planet, and wrote best-selling books on the subject.

More recently, powerful telescopes and visits by space probes have shown that the *canali* are natural features on the surface of the planet. English novelist HG Wells was inspired by the idea of Martian life, too, and wrote *The War of the Worlds* in 1896. This popular book tells the terrifying story of a Martian invasion.

In the 1920s, Mars was more popular than ever. Many people put forward schemes to look for evidence of life there.

One scheme even involved the US Army and Navy – they shut down their radio broadcasts and listened for radio communication from intelligent Martians. No signals were detected.

Another scheme involved shining bright searchlights up into space in the direction of Mars, to send a message to the planet's inhabitants.

Mars fever dwindled a little in the 1930s, but was given a boost in 1938 by American actor and film director Orson Welles. On 30 October that year, Welles broadcast a radio production of HG Wells' *The War of the Worlds*. Welles made the story sound as if it were a genuine news report. Thousands of Americans listening to the radio play believed that it was real, and panicked.

Nine years after Orson Welles' radio programme, the term 'flying saucer' was coined. It was 24 June 1947, and pilot Kenneth Arnold was flying home on his private jet. He saw a string of nine saucer-shaped objects that he could not identify. Arnold later described these unidentified flying objects (UFOs): 'They flew like a saucer would if you skimmed it across the water.'

THE ROSWELL INCIDENT

PERHAPS THE MOST FAMOUS UFO STORY IS THE ROSWELL INCIDENT, WHICH BEGAN JUST A WEEK AFTER KENNETH ARNOLD'S FLYING SAUCER SIGHTING.

ROSWELL

THE EVENTS CENTRED ON A TOWN CALLED ROSWELL IN NEW MEXICO, USA, WHERE FARM HAND W.W. 'MAC' BRAZEL FOUND SOME STRANGE FRAGMENTS OF METAL FOIL IN ONE OF HIS FIELDS.

THE US ARMY IMMEDIATELY ISSUED A REPORT THAT THE FRAGMENTS WERE DEBRIS FROM AN UNIDENTIFIED FLYING DISK.

HOWEVER, THE VERY NEXT DAY, THEY CHANGED THEIR STORY, AND CLAIMED THAT THE FOIL WAS FROM A CRASHED WEATHER BALLOON.

AROUND THAT TIME, THERE WERE MANY OTHER UFO SIGHTINGS ACROSS THE USA INCLUDING SEVERAL BY MILITARY PERSONNEL. SEVERAL OF THE SIGHTINGS WERE CONFIRMED BY RADAR.

25

ON THE SAME DAY THAT BRAZEL REPORTED HIS FOIL FRAGMENTS, A CIGAR-SHAPED CRAFT WAS REPORTED TO HAVE CRASHED IN THE DESERT ABOUT 110 KILOMETRES NORTHWEST OF ROSWELL.

THE AREA AROUND THE CRASH SITE WAS SOON SEALED OFF AND THE WHOLE MATTER BECAME HIGHLY CONFIDENTIAL. ANYONE INVOLVED WAS SWORN TO SECRECY.

TOP SECRET

SOME PEOPLE BELIEVE THAT ALIEN CREATURES WERE FOUND IN THE WRECKAGE.

THERE WERE EYEWITNESS REPORTS OF YELLOW-SKINNED CREATURES BEING REMOVED FROM THE WRECKAGE OF THE CRASHED OBJECT, AND TAKEN TO A NEARBY AIR BASE. IN THE 1990s, AN OLD PIECE OF FILM WAS DISCOVERED. THAT SEEMS TO SHOW TWO DEAD ALIEN CREATURES BEING ANALYSED BY POST MORTEM. EVEN IF THE FILM IS A HOAX, EYEWITNESS REPORTS OF THE POST MORTEMS ARE CONVINCING.

AS MANY AS 65% OF AMERICANS BELIEVE THAT IT WAS A UFO THAT CRASHED AT ROSWELL. SOME FORMER AIR FORCE EMPLOYEES HAVE GONE FURTHER: THEY INSIST THAT THE CRASHED CRAFT IS BEING HELD IN A TOP SECRET PART OF A NEW MEXICO AIR BASE KNOWN AS AREA 51. THEY ALSO CLAIM THAT UP TO EIGHT OTHER ALIEN CRAFT ARE BEING HELD THERE.

Flying saucer stories like the Roswell incident
caught people's imaginations. Soon there were
many other reports of UFOs. Some of the stories
involved sightings of, or even contact with, aliens.
These 'close encounters' are often categorised
into different kinds (more about this on pages
82 to 89).

In response to all the UFO sightings, the US Air Force set up top secret lists of all the UFO cases. The most famous of these lists was called Project Blue Book, which contained over ten thousand cases. Around 95% of the sightings could be explained as natural phenomena, aeroplanes or hoaxes. But what about the other 5%? Perhaps some people really have seen space craft from alien civilisations.

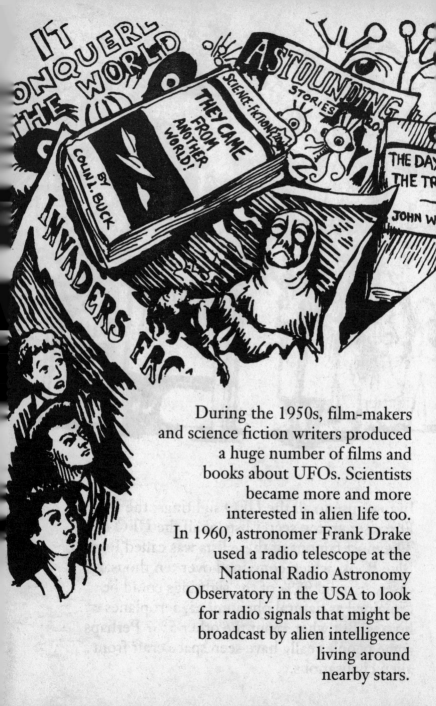

IT CONQUERED THE WORLD

ASTOUNDING STORIES

SCIENCE-FICTION

THEY CAME FROM ANOTHER WORLD!

BY COLIN L. BUCK

THE DAY THE TR—

JOHN W

INVADERS FRO

During the 1950s, film-makers and science fiction writers produced a huge number of films and books about UFOs. Scientists became more and more interested in alien life too. In 1960, astronomer Frank Drake used a radio telescope at the National Radio Astronomy Observatory in the USA to look for radio signals that might be broadcast by alien intelligence living around nearby stars.

Seven years later, in December 1967, an interesting radio signal from outer space was picked up by Jocelyn Bell.

On a printout from a radio telescope she was operating, Bell noticed a regular pulsing radio signal. Nothing like it had ever been seen: the pulses were coming every 1.3 seconds. The only explanation that Bell could find was that the signal must be from an intelligent civilisation, so she wrote 'LGM' – meaning 'Little Green Men' – on the printout. Unfortunately, it soon became clear that the signals were not from aliens at all. In fact, Bell had discovered a new type of object – a dying star called a pulsar.

The search continues for radio signals from intelligent aliens, but none has been found . . . yet. More about this on pages 50 to 53.

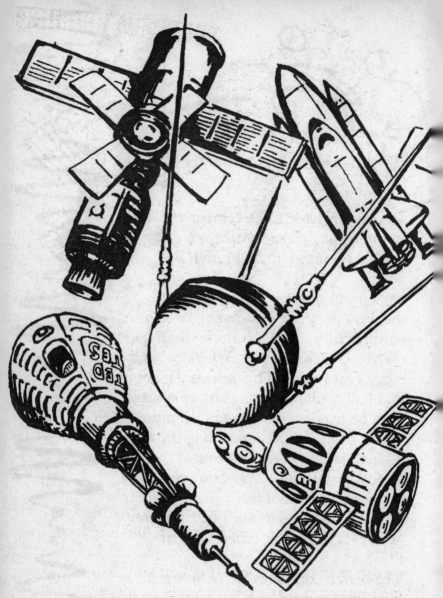

Another important development of the 1950s was space travel. The Space Age began on 4 October 1958, with the launch of the first human-made object in space, the Russian satellite, Sputnik.

But it was space probes, not satellites, that were to
be important in the search for alien life. A space
probe is a spacecraft, normally sent to another
planet, with special cameras and other scientific
instruments that take photographs or make
measurements. The information is beamed
back to Earth as radio signals, and space scientists
can then analyse the data to discover more about
the planet.

Some probes are 'landers', which actually land on a planet, as their name suggests. Earth people have sent landers to the Moon, Venus and Mars. Sometimes, these probes have been equipped with experiments to look for signs of life.

IT LOOKS PRETTY LIFELESS OUT THERE SIR.....

34

But no life has been found . . . yet.
(More about space probes on
pages 54 to 57.)

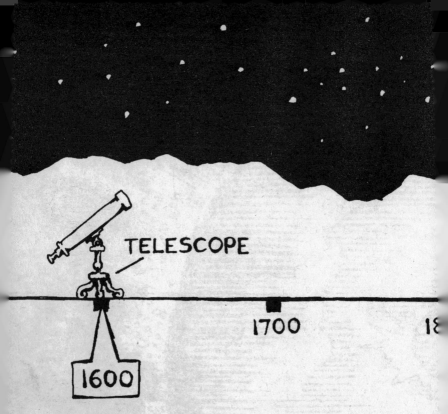

TELESCOPE

1700

18

1600

So, the idea that life might exist elsewhere in the Universe is at least 2,000 years old. But we have only had telescopes for 400 years. And only in the past 70 years have we had radio telescopes, the most likely source of proof that alien intelligence exists.

And only in the past 40 years or so have we made the first steps into space, where we may find the answers to the question 'Is there life out there?'. Perhaps in the next ten years we shall have an answer. Maybe the first signals are being picked up now, as you read this . . .

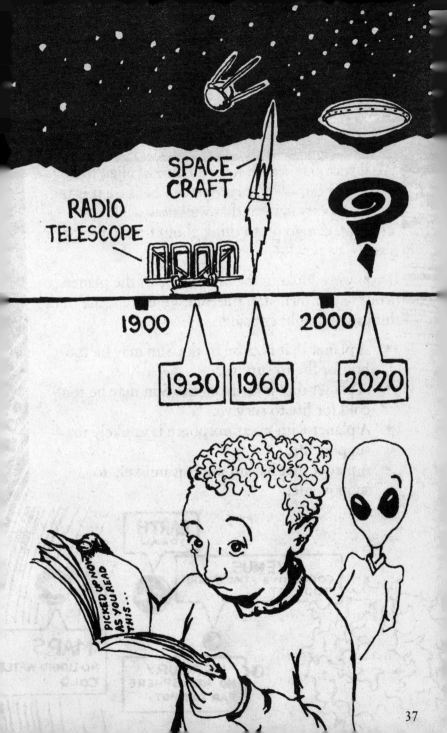

SPACE CRAFT

RADIO TELESCOPE

1900

2000

1930

1960

2020

PICKED UP NOW AS YOU READ THIS....

LOOKING FOR ALIEN LIFE

We'll start our search for evidence of alien life by looking at our own Solar System, because it is the only planetary system that we know well.
Then we can go on to think about life that might be further away.

If you were looking for life on one of the planets orbiting our own star, the Sun, here are some of the things you might consider:

- A planet that is close to the Sun may be too hot for life to survive.
- A planet that is far from the Sun may be too cold for life to survive.
- A planet with no atmosphere is unlikely to support life.
- A planet that has no water is unlikely to support life.

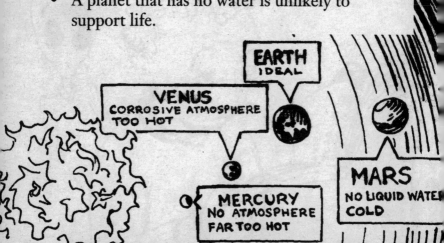

EARTH
IDEAL

VENUS
CORROSIVE ATMOSPHERE
TOO HOT

MERCURY
NO ATMOSPHERE
FAR TOO HOT

MARS
NO LIQUID WATER
COLD

Only one planet – Earth – stands out as a likely place for life to develop. And indeed, Earth is teeming with life . . . including intelligent creatures such as humans.

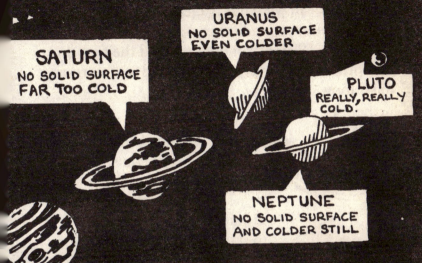

SATURN
NO SOLID SURFACE
FAR TOO COLD

URANUS
NO SOLID SURFACE
EVEN COLDER

PLUTO
REALLY, REALLY
COLD.

NEPTUNE
NO SOLID SURFACE
AND COLDER STILL

JUPITER
NO SOLID
SURFACE
TOO COLD

So, it seems unlikely, though not impossible, that life exists on the planets that we know. If life does exist in our Solar System, it may be more likely that it exists on the moons of the planets, or even on asteroids or comets (more about this on pages 58 to 61).

But now let's look further afield. There are about 100,000 million stars in our galaxy. Are there planets around them that might have life?

Stars appear just as dots of light when viewed through even the most powerful telescopes, so their planets would be too small to be seen. If we can't see them, how can we tell if planets really do exist around other stars? As recently as 1995, astronomers found the first proof that other stars do have planets, and it's interesting to see how.

Imagine that you are spinning around on one spot. Now imagine that as you spin, you are holding a heavy bag at arm's length. As the bag flies around you, you find it difficult to stand still on the same spot. The heavier the bag, the more you wobble. In a similar way, a heavy planet orbiting a star causes the star to wobble.

Astronomers measured the wobble of a star called 51 Pegasi, and proved that it has a planet in orbit around it. 51 Pegasi is almost identical to our Sun. Perhaps life lurks there, just 42 light years away. Several other planets have been discovered since 1995, and it is probably safe to assume that many stars have planets.

Is there any way to calculate how many planets in our galaxy are likely to have intelligent life? First, we'll try to find out how many planets there are. We just don't know how many stars have planets, but it is almost certainly not every star. So, let's begin by guessing that one in every 100 stars – about 1,000 million – have planets. Let's say that on average they have ten planets each. That's 10,000 million planets in our galaxy.

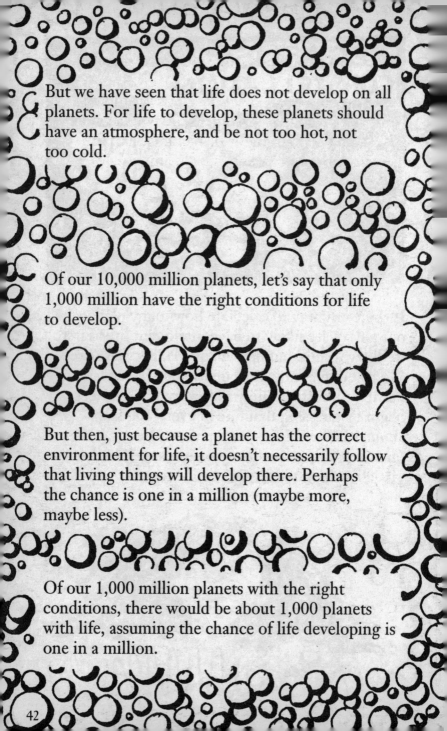

But we have seen that life does not develop on all planets. For life to develop, these planets should have an atmosphere, and be not too hot, not too cold.

Of our 10,000 million planets, let's say that only 1,000 million have the right conditions for life to develop.

But then, just because a planet has the correct environment for life, it doesn't necessarily follow that living things will develop there. Perhaps the chance is one in a million (maybe more, maybe less).

Of our 1,000 million planets with the right conditions, there would be about 1,000 planets with life, assuming the chance of life developing is one in a million.

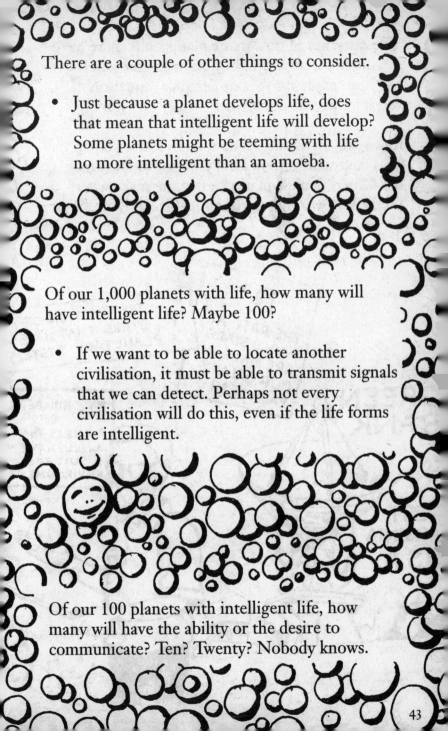

There are a couple of other things to consider.

- Just because a planet develops life, does that mean that intelligent life will develop? Some planets might be teeming with life no more intelligent than an amoeba.

Of our 1,000 planets with life, how many will have intelligent life? Maybe 100?

- If we want to be able to locate another civilisation, it must be able to transmit signals that we can detect. Perhaps not every civilisation will do this, even if the life forms are intelligent.

Of our 100 planets with intelligent life, how many will have the ability or the desire to communicate? Ten? Twenty? Nobody knows.

The question of how many planets out there have intelligent life that might want to communicate has been made into a mathematical equation. (If you hate maths, don't worry, this won't hurt.)

It's called the Drake Equation, after the person who devised it, Frank Drake. It is also known as the Green Bank Equation, after the place where Drake was working at the time: Green Bank, West Virginia, USA.

GREEN BANK

WEST VIRGINIA U.S.A.

R* THE RATE AT WHICH STARS ARE MADE IN OUR GALAXY EACH YEAR

fp THE FRACTION OF STARS THAT HAVE A PLANETARY SYSTEM

ne NUMBER OF PLANETS THAT WILL HAVE A SUITABLE ENVIRONMENT

The Drake equation is shown below.

All you really need to know about it is that the answer to the equation is a number, N. We have to write N rather than the actual number, because we don't know its value. N is the number of intelligent civilisations in our galaxy that might want to communicate. It's as simple as that.

All those other letters stand for other numbers that we need to use to find out what N is. (We don't know what those numbers are, either!)

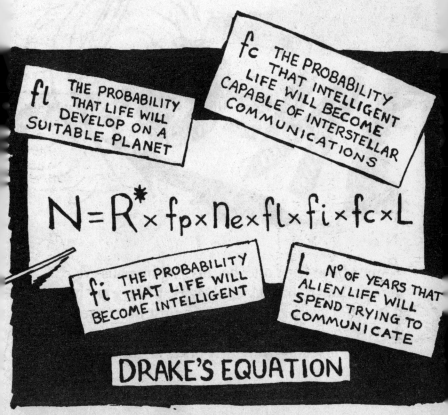

fc THE PROBABILITY THAT INTELLIGENT LIFE WILL BECOME CAPABLE OF INTERSTELLAR COMMUNICATIONS

fl THE PROBABILITY THAT LIFE WILL DEVELOP ON A SUITABLE PLANET

$$N = R^* \times fp \times Ne \times fl \times fi \times fc \times L$$

fi THE PROBABILITY THAT LIFE WILL BECOME INTELLIGENT

L Nº OF YEARS THAT ALIEN LIFE WILL SPEND TRYING TO COMMUNICATE

DRAKE'S EQUATION

We can only hazard wild guesses about most of the numbers in the Drake Equation, so we'll never work out an accurate answer. You might think 'What's the point of working out an equation like this if you don't know whether the answer will be 100, 1,000 or a million?' Well, believe it or not, that really doesn't matter. The important point is that we know that the answer, N, must be greater than zero. Can you see why?

N must be at least one, because we humans are here on Earth. But it's unlikely that N is exactly 1. If N is not zero, and is not 1, it must be greater than 1. So, looking at the Drake Equation logically, it seems likely that other civilisations do exist.

Although nobody knows the values of the numbers in the Drake Equation, many ET hunters have tried to estimate them. Some have suggested that the number N may be as small as one, others have worked out N to be about a million! Imagine one million civilisations in our galaxy. The most popular answer for many experts seems to be about one thousand. What do you think?

So, once we have thought about how many other civilisations there might be, how do we go about finding them? If we sent out a spacecraft to the nearest star, the journey would take tens or hundreds of years. And what if the star you visited had no life around it? That would be a bit of a wasted journey.

Because the space between any two stars is so
great, the simplest way for intelligent life to
make contact is to send out signals. The best
signals to use for this are radio waves, because
they pass straight through the dust and gas
that is found in huge patches here and there in
space. So, assuming that other civilisations
realise this, the most sensible way to look for
extra-terrestrial intelligence is to search the
sky for radio signals.

There is a problem: lots of things in space give out radio waves. So, how could we tell whether a radio signal is from a star, a galaxy or an alien civilisation? To make its presence felt, an alien civilisation would have to send out signals that follow a different pattern from the radio waves given out by stars.

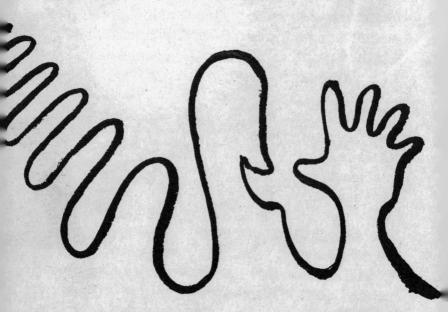

This is why Jocelyn Bell thought that the strange signal she picked up from her radio telescope was coming from little green men (see page 31). Bell's signal turned out not to be a message from aliens, and the search is still on for signals that have been created by intelligent creatures.

An organisation called the SETI Institute is one of the groups at the forefront of this search for messages from outer space. The letters SETI stand for the Search for Extraterrestrial Intelligence. The SETI Institute is based in California, USA.

One of SETI's founders is none other than Frank Drake, creator of the Drake Equation. Drake was the first to use a radio telescope to look for intelligent extraterrestrials, in April 1960. This was the beginning of Project Ozma, in which Drake and his colleagues studied a 'nearby' star (only about 10,000 million million kilometres away), using their radio telescope. No intelligent signals were detected.

There have been about 60 similar searches since Project Ozma, but none has so far found any evidence of alien intelligence.

One of the problems with looking for intelligent radio signals is that radio waves come to us at many different frequencies.

Back in the 1960s, people using radio telescopes to search for intelligent signals had to tune into one particular frequency at a time, just as you tune in an ordinary radio to your favourite station.

Nowadays, with the help of a powerful computer, SETI telescopes scan the sky at many different wavelengths, searching for that elusive 'Hello' from a cosmic DJ.

The amount of data from this search is vast, and analysis of the signals is carried out by computers. In 1997, a project called SETI@home was set up by a group of scientists calling themselves BIGSCIENCE, working with an organisation called SERENDIP at University College Berkeley in the USA. The idea is to have thousands of personal computers all over the world working on the data at the same time. Signals detected by the radio telescope are sent via the Internet to the PCs, and the analysis is sent back to a computer at project SERENDIP.

While we wait for the signals to come flooding in from the SETI people, space scientists are still looking for life elsewhere in the Solar System – on other planets and their moons.

We can tell a lot about a planet by looking at it from Earth, using telescopes and other equipment. We can tell what atmospheric conditions are like on the planet, and what chemical compounds are present. But no telescope is powerful enough to see whether anything is alive on the planet.

The best way to find out if life is to be found on a
planet is to go there, and that's where space
probes come in.

A space probe is a robotic spacecraft that carries
cameras and scientific equipment that can help
to find out more about a planet. Probes are
controlled from Earth by radio signals.
It's a bit like using a remote
controlled model aeroplane,
but at a distance of several
million kilometres.
The most exciting probes
are the ones that land on
the surface of a planet,
collecting and
analysing samples
of soil or rock.

A few probes have successfully landed on the Moon and Mars. In some cases, the probes carried out experiments on the rocks and soil to test for life.

In 1976, two Viking lander probes set down on the surface of Mars in 1976. Experiments on board the probes tested soil that was scooped up from the surface, to see whether there were any chemical signs of life. The experiment seemed to suggest that there was no life on Mars.

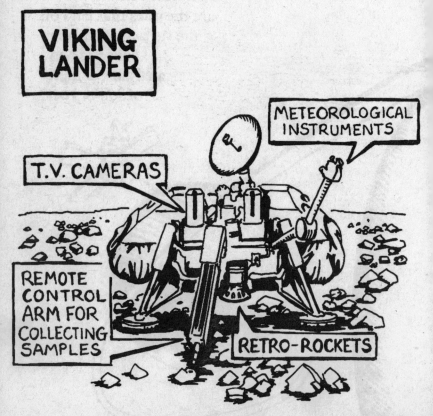

VIKING LANDER

METEOROLOGICAL INSTRUMENTS

T.V. CAMERAS

REMOTE CONTROL ARM FOR COLLECTING SAMPLES

RETRO-ROCKETS

More probes will be sent to Mars, and some of them will perform different experiments to search for signs of life. Perhaps life existed there millions of years ago and has long since disappeared. Experiments aboard some future probes will look for evidence of that. Only when astronauts visit the planet – perhaps as early as 2010 – will we know for sure whether life has ever existed on Mars.

So it seems unlikely that any planets other than Earth in our Solar System support life. But perhaps life might be found on comets, asteroids, or moons. There are moons orbiting most of the planets, just as the Moon orbits the Earth. Unfortunately, most of the moons in the Solar System do not have atmospheres, so there's probably no life there.

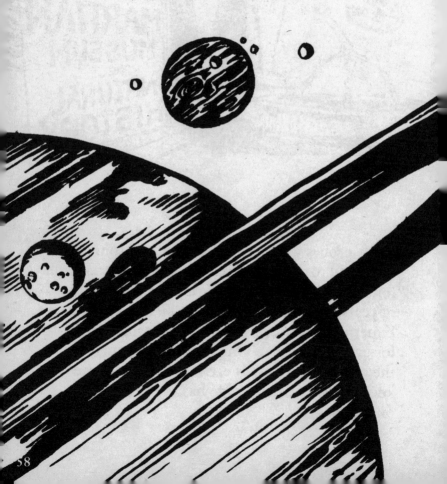

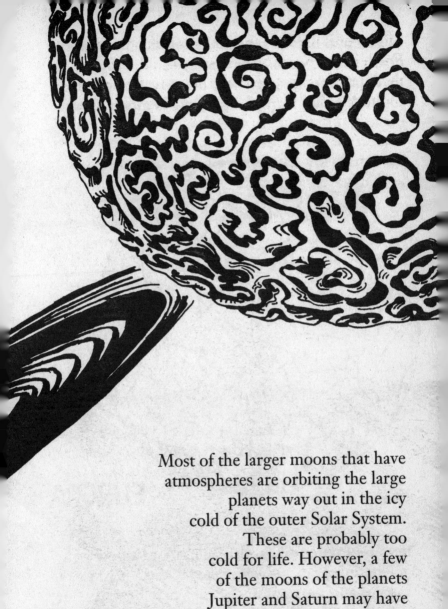

Most of the larger moons that have
atmospheres are orbiting the large
planets way out in the icy
cold of the outer Solar System.
These are probably too
cold for life. However, a few
of the moons of the planets
Jupiter and Saturn may have
some surprises in store.

Jupiter and Saturn are so far from the Sun that the planets and their moons are very cold. However, there are two moons where life may yet be found: Jupiter's moon Europa and Saturn's moon Titan.

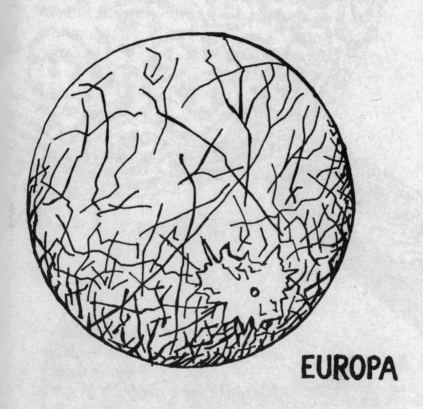

EUROPA

Because Jupiter is a large planet, it has a strong gravitational pull, which stretches and squashes Europa and warms it up. Europa may be warm enough to have huge oceans of liquid water, ammonia or methane. Perhaps there are primitive living creatures swimming around in them.

The orange clouds of Titan have been found to consist of chemicals that are necessary for life as we know it, which may be very similar to Earth's. Perhaps there are creatures living on Titan, adapted to the extreme cold conditions there. A space probe called Cassini set off for Saturn and its moons in 1997, carrying a small separate probe (Huygens) that would crash land on Titan, looking to see if conditions are right for life.

Of course, planets around other stars may have moons, too. If they do, this increases the chance of life elsewhere in the galaxy, and makes the number N in the Drake equation bigger.

TITAN

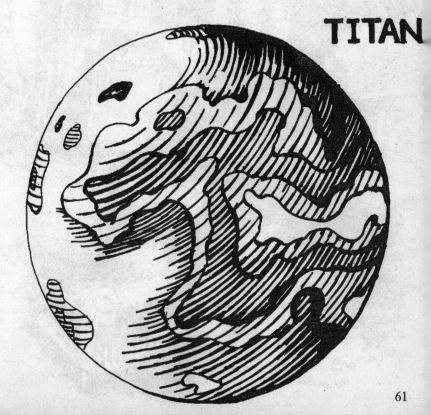

WHAT MIGHT ALIEN LIFE BE LIKE ?

Eventually, every possible nook or cranny in the Solar System where life could possibly be found will be investigated. If we find alien life in our own Solar System, what might it be like? And what about life outside the Solar System? Would we even recognise it as life if it was sitting in the same room?

If a space probe went to collect samples from a planet and returned them to Earth, how would we know whether there was any life in the sample?

What makes some things alive and others not alive? Have you ever wondered why a dog is alive but a rock is not? Why are bacteria alive but not a computer? Living things are not necessarily intelligent, and they don't necessarily have legs or eyes. So, what makes something alive?

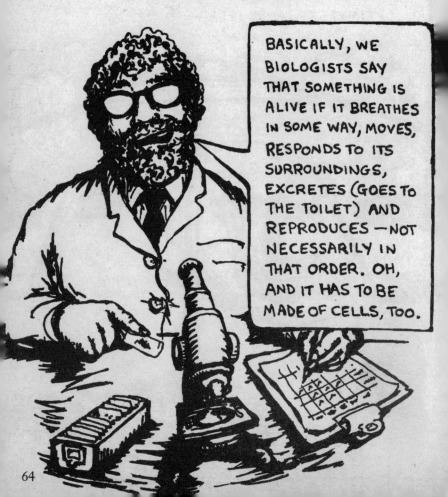

BASICALLY, WE BIOLOGISTS SAY THAT SOMETHING IS ALIVE IF IT BREATHES IN SOME WAY, MOVES, RESPONDS TO ITS SURROUNDINGS, EXCRETES (GOES TO THE TOILET) AND REPRODUCES — NOT NECESSARILY IN THAT ORDER. OH, AND IT HAS TO BE MADE OF CELLS, TOO.

The chemistry of life as we know it is based on the chemical element carbon. Atoms of carbon join together to form long chains or other huge complex molecules. These are called organic molecules.

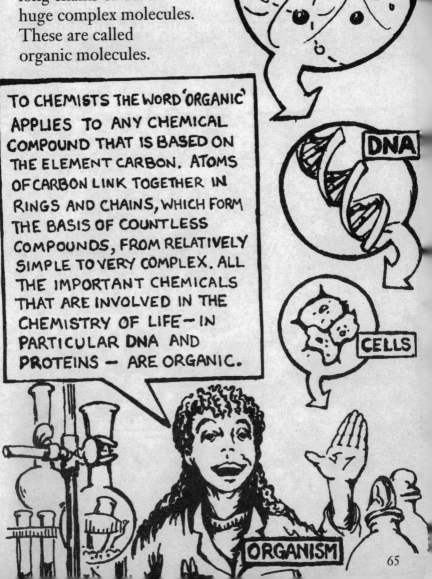

CARBON AND OTHER ATOMS

DNA

CELLS

ORGANISM

TO CHEMISTS THE WORD 'ORGANIC' APPLIES TO ANY CHEMICAL COMPOUND THAT IS BASED ON THE ELEMENT CARBON. ATOMS OF CARBON LINK TOGETHER IN RINGS AND CHAINS, WHICH FORM THE BASIS OF COUNTLESS COMPOUNDS, FROM RELATIVELY SIMPLE TO VERY COMPLEX. ALL THE IMPORTANT CHEMICALS THAT ARE INVOLVED IN THE CHEMISTRY OF LIFE — IN PARTICULAR DNA AND PROTEINS — ARE ORGANIC.

So, life on Earth is based on the element carbon, and we recognise it because it reproduces, moves, is made of cells and so on. Would alien life be based on carbon? We can only guess, but it is an educated guess. We need to call in an exobiologist — a biologist who specialises in the possibility of alien life.

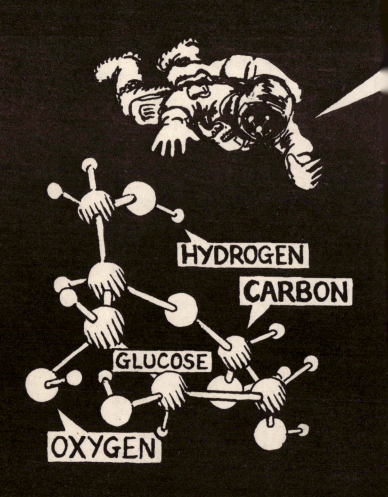

HYDROGEN

CARBON

GLUCOSE

OXYGEN

ANY TYPE OF LIFE MUST BE A PROCESS INVOLVING COMPLEX CHEMICAL COMPOUNDS. THE ELEMENTS THAT WE KNOW ON EARTH ARE THE SAME ONES AS THE WHOLE UNIVERSE IS MADE OF, SO WE HAVE AROUND 90 TO CHOOSE FROM. THE ONLY ELEMENT OTHER THAN CARBON THAT CAN FORM COMPLEX COMPOUNDS THAT MIGHT BE THE BASIS OF LIFE IS SILICON, AND SOME PEOPLE HAVE SUGGESTED THAT ALIEN LIFE MIGHT BE BASED ON SILICON. WE NEED TO TALK TO A CHEMIST ABOUT THIS.

IT'S ME AGAIN. SILICON AS THE BASIS FOR LIFE ON EARTH? WELL, THERE IS CERTAINLY LOTS OF SILICON IN THE UNIVERSE. IT IS ONE OF THE MOST ABUNDANT ELEMENTS ON EARTH, FOR EXAMPLE. AND IT CAN FORM RINGS AND CHAINS, JUST LIKE CARBON CAN. HOWEVER, ABOVE TEMPERATURES OF ABOUT -200°CELSIUS THESE RINGS BREAK DOWN. SO, THERE MAY BE STRANGE CREATURES BASED ON SILICON ON SOME FARAWAY PLANET THAT IS VERY COLD.

So if it exists, alien life will probably be based on the element carbon or the element silicon. But, even if carbon-based life exists elsewhere, it will probably not be familiar to us.

The features of living things on Earth have arisen by evolution: a long, slow process by which living things adapt to their environment. Feathers, leaves, flowers, legs, feet and eyes, and even blood and bones, have evolved over millions of years in the particular conditions found here on Earth. So it's unlikely that on other planets there are creatures which look like donkeys or slugs. Flowers and trees are likely to be unique to Earth too.

So alien life probably wouldn't look anything like the plants and animals that we know. And it is even less likely to resemble human beings. Jack Cohen, an evolutionary biologist and author, says that he doesn't believe UFO stories about little green men — not because they are little and green, but because they are men! It is unlikely, though not impossible, that aliens would be humanoid, as they so often are described in stories of close encounters.

Can we make any guesses about what alien life might look like? Living things on other planets will probably have evolved to suit their environment, as they have done on Earth. But the conditions on other planets or moons are likely to be quite different to those on Earth, so any life there would also be very different. Life on Earth depends on a mixture of nitrogen, oxygen, carbon dioxide and water vapour, but another planet's atmosphere might contain lots of methane and ammonia gases, or a mist of sulphuric acid.

A large planet has a stronger gravitational pull than a small one. Creatures living on such a planet wouldn't

survive well with long, thin legs. Perhaps small creatures would evolve there.

Sulphuric acid can be highly corrosive. On a planet with sulphuric acid in the atmosphere, no creature like any on Earth would survive. A thick,

outer covering would be a must for any living thing there.

Some planets have no real surface at all — they are made of gases. Jupiter and Saturn are examples of such 'gas giants' in our own Solar System. Living things on this planet would have to be buoyant, like a hot air balloon, or have wings to stop themselves from falling down to the hot, dense centre of the planet.

There are creatures living on Earth that might help us to predict what alien life might be like. These strange creatures are called extremophiles, which means they live in extreme conditions.

For example, there are tiny animals living inside some volcanoes. These organisms are quite different from any other life on Earth. Their staple diet consists mainly of sulphur and lots of heat. These are the sort of conditions that might exist on a planet or a moon somewhere.

Strange life forms have been found living near underwater volcanoes known as black smokers on Earth. Similar volcanoes might be found on Jupiter's moon Europa. There may be life in vast oceans hidden below Europa's cracked surface.

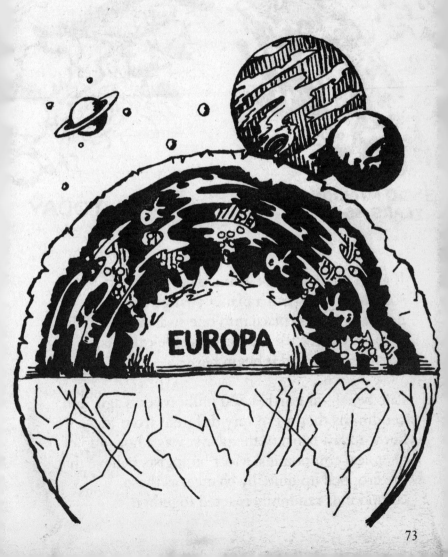

EUROPA

EARTH

3500 MILLION YEARS AGO

TODAY

If alien life does exist, it must have started somehow. How can a planet change from a desolate, lifeless place into one swarming with life? The only place we are sure that life exists is on Earth, so how did it begin here?

Life began on Earth 3,500 million years ago, and conditions then were very different from those we know today. Most of the planet was a hot soup of chemical compounds. Most biologists believe that life cropped up quite by chance, as these compounds randomly reacted together.

Since the 1920s, various experiments have been carried out in an attempt to recreate the conditions of the early Earth, to see whether life could be created in a glass jar. In a famous experiment in the 1950s, Stanley Miller filled a laboratory flask with a mixture of chemicals like those on the early Earth, and added energy by producing sparks of electricity in the flask. After just a few days, many of the complex organic substances that are essential to life were formed.

THE MILLER-UREY EXPERIMENT

METHANE
AMMONIA
HYDROGEN

ORGANIC MOLECULES COLLECT HERE

SPARK

WATER

HEAT

CONDENSER

The chemicals that were in the soup of the early Earth are common in the Solar System, and probably on planets around other stars. So, could the chemicals necessary for life have been produced elsewhere?

Using a clever technique called spectroscopy, astronomers have identified organic molecules on asteroids and comets. Some space scientists have even suggested that life on Earth began when a comet collided with our planet long ago, bringing with it the complex chemicals, ready-made.

But the ingredients of life are not the same as life itself. And life is not the same as intelligent life.

Human beings – the only creatures on Earth capable of understanding and exploring outer space – did not appear until more than 3,000 million years after life first began. In that time, life on a planet can be wiped out in a number of ways. Perhaps the chance of intelligent life having time to develop is extremely small, and we just got lucky?

So, if other planets have the correct chemical ingredients for life, *and* a good environment for life to develop, *and* the right chemical reactions take place, life will begin there. But it may not be anything like we expect, and it may not be intelligent.

If alien life exists far away, outside our Solar System, then we shall not find it for many years. For now, we shall have to rely upon its finding us. Perhaps they already have. Could some of the UFO reports be true?

HAVE WE BEEN VISITED BY ALIENS?

If alien creatures discovered planet Earth, and realised that it had the correct temperature and chemical composition for life to begin, they would probably want to visit the planet and search for life there.

When they found it, they would want to study it, and would probably want to remain undercover. So, it could be that intelligent extraterrestrials have already found us and have paid us a visit.

If aliens have visited Earth, perhaps some of the UFO stories are true. Most UFO sightings are shown to be weather-related, military aeroplanes, the planet Venus in the early evening sky, or simply hoaxes.

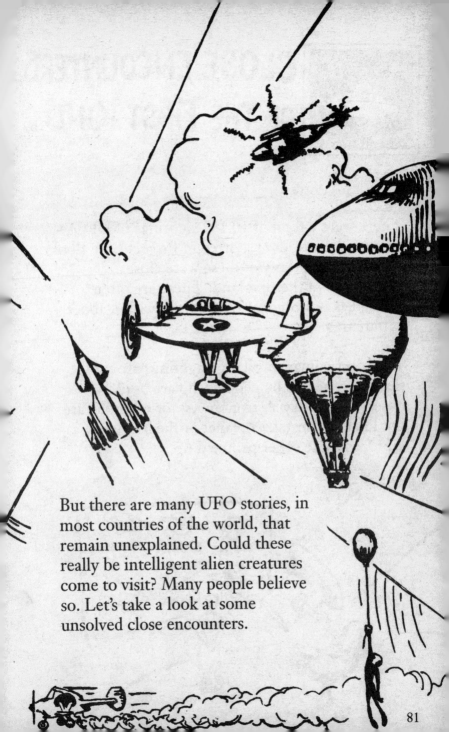

But there are many UFO stories, in most countries of the world, that remain unexplained. Could these really be intelligent alien creatures come to visit? Many people believe so. Let's take a look at some unsolved close encounters.

CLOSE ENCOUNTERS
OF THE FIRST KIND.

There were a total of 10,147 sightings of UFOs –
all over the world – reported in Project Blue Book
(see page 29). Many of these were close
encounters of the first kind. These are often
defined as sightings of UFOs from within about
150 metres.

The most convincing UFO sightings are those
that are reported by people who are used to
observing the sky. Astronomers, for example, are
not likely to mistake a planet or the Moon for a
UFO, as some other people do.

Close encounters are also convincing when many people report the same thing. In 1977, the entire crew of a Russian Navy ship, the Volga, saw nine UFOs. The strange objects carried out complicated manoeuvres around the ship for eighteen minutes.

CLOSE ENCOUNTERS OF THE SECOND KIND.

Some UFO sightings are accompanied by physical evidence of some sort, such as detection by radar or a disturbance of electrical power. These are close encounters of the second kind.

During the UFO sighting aboard the Volga, for example, all radio communications were lost. Other sorts of physical evidence of UFOs include crop circles and disturbance to sand, soil, or even ice.

The crew aboard another Russian ship reported seeing a brilliantly-lit spherical object break through the ice and rise up through the air. This left a unique piece of physical evidence – a huge hole in the ice.

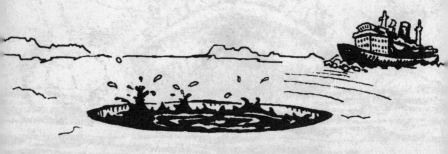

In recent years, mysterious geometrical patterns have been found cut into growing corn in farmers' fields. Some people believe that these 'crop circles' are created by intelligent alien creatures. Often when a crop circle is discovered, it turns out that there have been UFO sightings in the area around that time.

Most people think that crop circles are elaborate hoaxes, but some people believe they are evidence of alien visits.

CLOSE ENCOUNTERS
OF THE THIRD KIND

In some cases, people actually report seeing alien beings, often standing at the portholes of their spacecraft or outside their spaceships. These are close encounters of the third kind.

4963 AL

CASE Nº	4963 AL		
HEIGHT	1·2 m	AGE	600
DISTINGUISHING FEATURES		GLOWS IN THE DARK	

Normally, when people talk about what they saw after such an encounter, they describe the alien creatures as humanoid, with two legs, a head, two big eyes and so on. It's very unlikely that alien beings would look anything like humans, so this makes sceptics think that the reports are made up or based on vivid dreams.

But perhaps many people really have seen aliens from the same race - a race that just happens to be humanoid. That would explain why all the descriptions of alien sightings are so similar.

CLOSE ENCOUNTERS OF THE FOURTH KIND.

A small proportion of close encounters involve what is called alien abduction. Either voluntarily or against their will, people are taken by aliens, sometimes for a period of several days. Normally, the people report being studied aboard alien craft, in rooms like hi-tech operating theatres.

One of the most famous close encounters of the fourth kind was made into a film, *Fire in the Sky*. The film tells the amazing story of an American logger, Travis Walton.

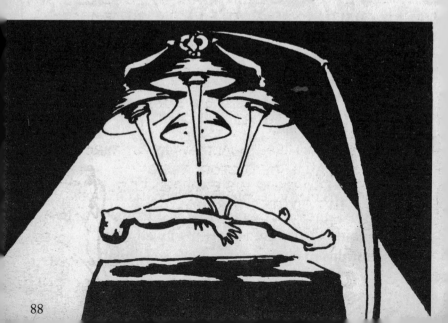

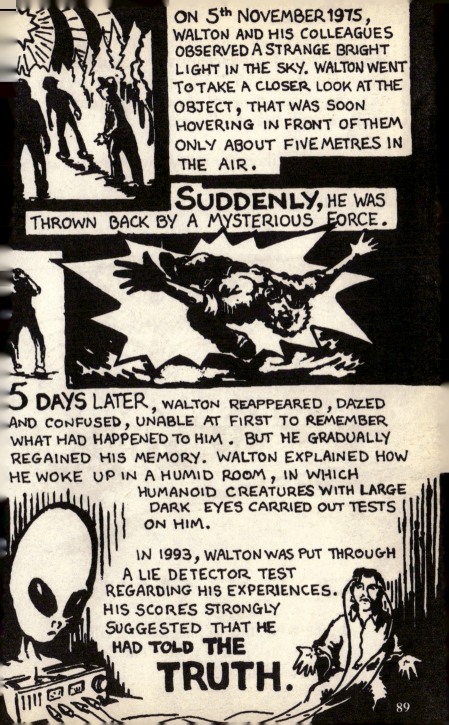

ON 5th NOVEMBER 1975, WALTON AND HIS COLLEAGUES OBSERVED A STRANGE BRIGHT LIGHT IN THE SKY. WALTON WENT TO TAKE A CLOSER LOOK AT THE OBJECT, THAT WAS SOON HOVERING IN FRONT OF THEM ONLY ABOUT FIVE METRES IN THE AIR.

SUDDENLY, HE WAS THROWN BACK BY A MYSTERIOUS FORCE.

5 DAYS LATER, WALTON REAPPEARED, DAZED AND CONFUSED, UNABLE AT FIRST TO REMEMBER WHAT HAD HAPPENED TO HIM. BUT HE GRADUALLY REGAINED HIS MEMORY. WALTON EXPLAINED HOW HE WOKE UP IN A HUMID ROOM, IN WHICH HUMANOID CREATURES WITH **LARGE** DARK EYES CARRIED OUT TESTS ON HIM.

IN 1993, WALTON WAS PUT THROUGH A LIE DETECTOR TEST REGARDING HIS EXPERIENCES. HIS SCORES STRONGLY SUGGESTED THAT HE HAD **TOLD THE TRUTH.**

All the stories of alien visitation we have looked at so far are from the 20th century. But there's no reason why aliens would wait until now to pay us a visit. Is there any evidence of visitations from hundreds or thousands of years ago?

It turns out that there are many unexplained sightings of objects in the sky from throughout history. Here are three of the best-known examples.

In the Bible, the prophet Ezekiel talks about lights in the sky, which he describes as clouds of fire.

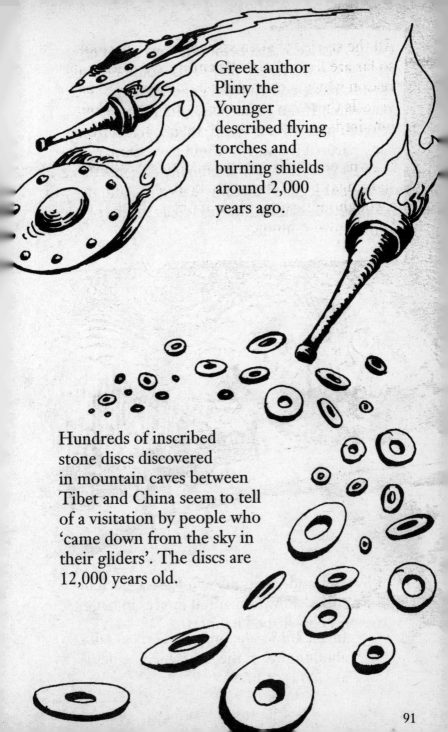

Greek author Pliny the Younger described flying torches and burning shields around 2,000 years ago.

Hundreds of inscribed stone discs discovered in mountain caves between Tibet and China seem to tell of a visitation by people who 'came down from the sky in their gliders'. The discs are 12,000 years old.

If aliens visited Earth before the invention of writing, the stories of their visits would become legends, passed down from generation to generation. If the aliens had visited several different parts of the world, then legends from many parts of the world would have similar features. It turns out that in many cultures there are ancient legends that involve eggs. And many of these legends can be interpreted as stories of alien visitors. For example . . .

• In Switzerland, Australia and Russia, ancient wall paintings show humanoid figures in baggy outfits and egg-shaped helmets.

• In Peru, South America, there is an ancient story of people emerging from gold and silver eggs that fell from the sky.

• In Japan, small ancient statues of humanoid figures have been found. The figures are wearing what look like egg-shaped helmets.

Perhaps alien creatures visited our planet long ago, in egg-shaped spaceships? Or perhaps the similarity between these egg stories is just coincidence.

Sometimes, people claim to have had direct communication with intelligent alien beings. This is often called a close encounter of the fifth kind.

One example involves an American woman, Marge Ludeman. For many years until her death in the 1980s, Ludeman 'received' more than 500 pages of messages from an alien commander-in-chief called 'Hilarion'. Ludeman claimed that the messages were dictated to her telepathically from outer space. The messages were composed in rhyme.

In a letter to the then President of the USA, Ronald Reagan, Hilarion explains – through Ludeman – that its race is living in great 'ships above Earth's troubled face'. It goes on to say that 'making physical contact is hard for us to do: only those whom we long ago sent to Earth can we use'. Hilarion also hinted that the alien race would like to land on Earth: 'A peaceful landing we would like to make, and not be greeted with distrust, fear or hate.'

There are a great many UFO sightings that remain unexplained. However, no close encounter – whether of the first, second, third, fourth or fifth kind – has ever been shown to be true without any doubt. There is no solid evidence that we have been visited by aliens.

Some people think that governments – in particular the US government – have already found aliens, but are covering up the stories. Why would they do this? Perhaps because they think there would be chaos if the news got out? If you were a world leader and an alien spacecraft was found in your country, what would you do? Would you keep it a secret, or tell the world?

There is still no definite evidence that alien life exists. Perhaps the best scientific evidence so far for alien life is the detection of complex organic molecules on comets and asteroids. The fact that the chemical compounds necessary for life exist elsewhere makes it seem more likely that life itself exists elsewhere, too.

There is another way that alien life might have visited Earth. It could have come by accident!

Small chunks of rock from space, called meteoroids, constantly bombard Earth. When they land, they are called meteorites.

In December 1984, a meteorite was found in the Arctic snow. It was given the name ALH84001 and stored away with thousands of others. Nearly ten years later, in 1993, it was taken out of storage, because space scientists realised that it was from Mars. It was analysed for three years by NASA scientists in America. The rock was found to have tiny marks in it that looked as though they had been left by tiny creatures – they looked like tiny fossils. Also, complex organic chemicals were found in the meteorite.

Three years later, in 1996, NASA decided to release details of the Martian meteorite. The newspapers said that scientists had proved that life exists on Mars. Was this really the first hard evidence of life on Mars?

Perhaps there was once life on Mars, but it died out millions of years ago. Liquid water probably once flowed over the surface of Mars, and life could perhaps have thrived there long ago. But the evidence in the meteorite was inconclusive. We still can't be sure if there was ever life on Mars.

MAKING CONTACT WITH ALIENS.

You may think that Marge Ludeman's telepathic messages from Hilarion the alien (see pages 94-95) were just made up. And they probably were. But what would happen if we really did make contact with aliens? Would we greet them with distrust, fear and hate, or welcome them with open arms? If we do find alien life – or if it finds us – will we be able to communicate with it at all?

When two people meet who do not speak the same languages, they cannot talk freely to each other. But they can still communicate, using their hands and facial expressions, for example. Human gestures such as smiles or frowns mean much the same everywhere on Earth – actions speak louder than words. But what would a smile mean to an alien? Probably nothing.

Even if you could somehow communicate with an alien, what would you talk about?

It is important that the people of the world think about what we should do if we receive a signal from outer space. The following extracts come from a scientific paper written in 1996 for the International Academy of Astronautics.

If SETI is successful in detecting an extraterrestrial civilisation, it will raise the question of whether and how humanity should attempt to communicate with the other civilisation. How should that decision be made? What should be the content of the message? Who should decide?

The paper proposes a set of principles to be followed when and if the time comes to send a message.

1. The decision on whether or not to send a message to extraterrestrial intelligence should be made by an appropriate international body, broadly representative of Humankind.

2. If a decision is made to send a message to extraterrestrial intelligence, it should be sent on behalf of all Humankind, rather than from individual States or groups.

3. The content of such a message should be developed through an appropriate international process, reflecting a broad consensus.

We may have already been communicating with aliens without even knowing it. Some radio waves that are supposed to carry radio and television broadcasts to homes on Earth escape into space. So, a constant stream of 'spare' radio signals has been travelling out into space for about one hundred years (since the invention of radio).

These signals could be detected on a planet far away. By examining them, intelligent aliens would realise that they had come from an intelligent civilisation. They might even be able to decode the signals, and listen to our radio broadcasts and watch our TV programmes.

Do you think that aliens around some nearby star might now be sitting down to dinner watching Australian soap operas? Or just keeping up with world events? Radio waves travel through space at the same speed as light. So, a civilisation that is 40 light years away would now be receiving programmes that were broadcast 40 years ago, because the signals that carry the programmes take 40 years to reach them.

Sadly, it is unlikely that these radio signals have been detected by alien civilisations. They are not sent in any particular direction, so the signals spread out as they travel through space, becoming extremely weak. And the further a civilisation is from Earth, the weaker the signals will be. Such weak signals would be drowned out by radio waves emitted by the Sun.

105

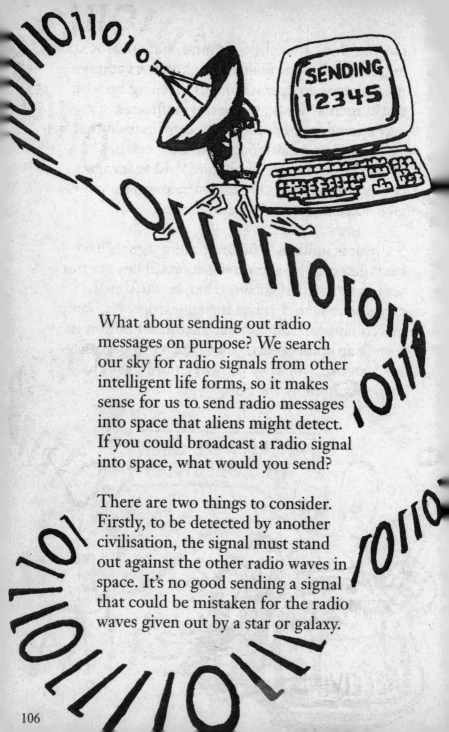

What about sending out radio messages on purpose? We search our sky for radio signals from other intelligent life forms, so it makes sense for us to send radio messages into space that aliens might detect. If you could broadcast a radio signal into space, what would you send?

There are two things to consider. Firstly, to be detected by another civilisation, the signal must stand out against the other radio waves in space. It's no good sending a signal that could be mistaken for the radio waves given out by a star or galaxy.

Secondly, you have to think about the content of the message. It is probably safe to assume that beings intelligent enough to look for and receive radio signals would understand the principles of mathematics. And maths is a universal language – for example, whatever you choose to name it, 'one' is always one more than 'zero'.

So, maths could be important in our communication with alien intelligences. A message that contains a sequence of numbers, for example, would certainly attract the attention of an alien expert.

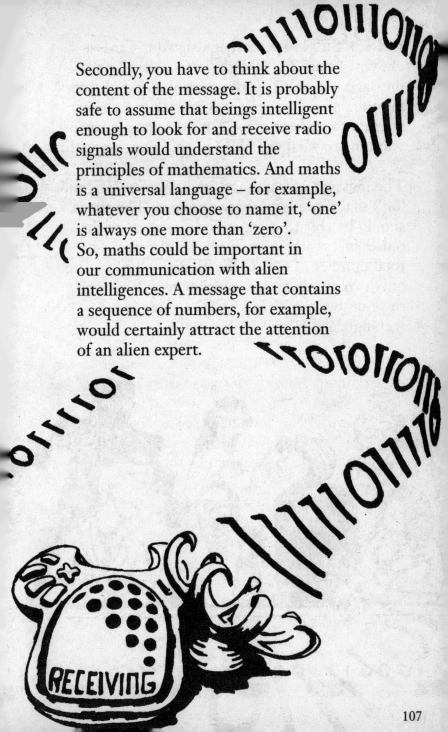

RECEIVING

In 1974, SETI experts sent a signal towards a cluster of stars 24,000 light years away. The message was only broadcast for a period of three minutes, so the exercise was not really a serious attempt to make contact. On the opposite page you can see what the SETI people came up with.

The message uses pulses of radio waves ('off' and 'on') that represent binary numbers. The aliens should be able to work out how to arrange the pulses in a rectangle to form the pictures. The total number of dots in the picture is 1,679. The only two numbers that multiply together to give this number are 23 and 73. The sides of the rectangle are 23 and 73 dots long.

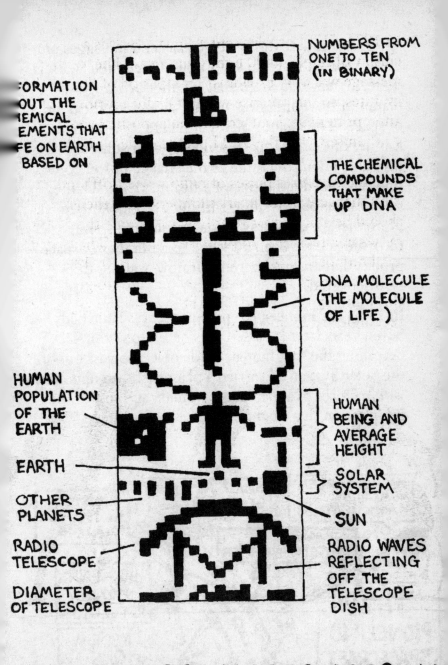

NUMBERS FROM ONE TO TEN (IN BINARY)

FORMATION OUT THE HEMICAL EMENTS THAT FE ON EARTH BASED ON

THE CHEMICAL COMPOUNDS THAT MAKE UP DNA

DNA MOLECULE (THE MOLECULE OF LIFE)

HUMAN POPULATION OF THE EARTH

HUMAN BEING AND AVERAGE HEIGHT

EARTH

SOLAR SYSTEM

OTHER PLANETS

SUN

RADIO TELESCOPE

RADIO WAVES REFLECTING OFF THE TELESCOPE DISH

DIAMETER OF TELESCOPE

OOOIIOIOOOOIIIIOIOIOOIIOOOIII

There is another way that we can send messages out into space – aboard space probes. Once their work is done, probes remain in space, either orbiting a planet or travelling ever further away into the depths of space. The chance of any intelligent creature ever finding one of our space probes is almost zero – probably about the same as the chance of someone finding a needle the size of a flea in a haystack the size of the Solar System, without even looking for it. Nonetheless, diagrams, photographs and sound recordings have been attached to a number of space probes that are out there right now, waiting to be discovered.

In 1972, the Pioneer 10 space probe was launched. Seven years later it passed outside Pluto's orbit – becoming the first human-made object to pass out of the Solar System. It carried a plaque (shown opposite) with pictures of a man and a woman, and some other information that might interest a passing alien.

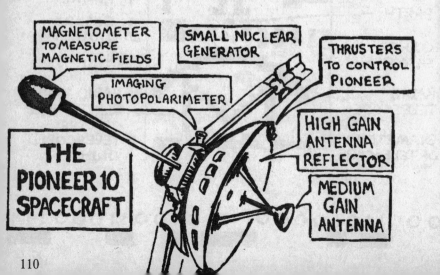

MAGNETOMETER TO MEASURE MAGNETIC FIELDS

SMALL NUCLEAR GENERATOR

THRUSTERS TO CONTROL PIONEER

IMAGING PHOTOPOLARIMETER

THE PIONEER 10 SPACECRAFT

HIGH GAIN ANTENNA REFLECTOR

MEDIUM GAIN ANTENNA

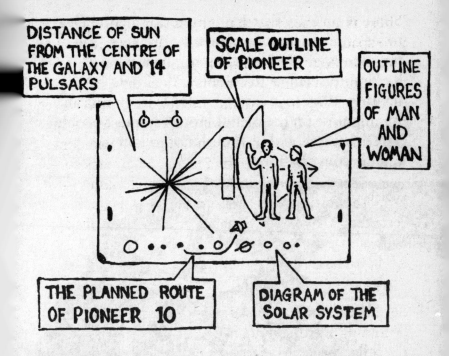

The Voyager space probes, launched in 1977, carried pictures and sounds, recorded onto a videodisk. The pictures included photographs of people from across the world, and of the Earth taken from space. The sounds included animal noises such as the trumpet of an elephant and the songs of birds. There was music and greetings from many different countries, too, and even the sound of a kiss. But there was no videodisk player attached to the probe. What sort of plug would you put on it, anyway?

Some people say that it might not be a good idea to let other civilisations know we are here. The message might be picked up by aliens who are looking for planets to colonise. We might be inviting dangerous extraterrestrials to dinner, and we might be on the menu! However, most people agree that it would be foolish not to join in a cosmic conversation.

Several SETI experts suggest that, instead of radio waves, light or infrared are the best type of radiation to use as the basis of any signals. The radiation could be produced by a powerful laser, and directed accurately to different destinations in the sky. The signals could be similar to those on the Internet. It could be that some kind of communications network like the Internet is already established in our galaxy, and that we are just the last civilisation to get connected.

LOCAL CALLS ▼   INTERNATIONAL CALLS ▼   INTERSTELLAR CALLS ▼

If we get connected in the next one hundred years or so, will we have anything interesting to say?

Another problem with communicating with extraterrestrials is that any messages we do send to alien civilisations will not be received for a long time. Based on the popular figure of 1,000 intelligent civilisations in our galaxy, the average distance between any two of them would be about 3,000 light years. Even if the distance to the nearest civilisation is just 100 light years away, imagine how difficult it would be to have a meaningful conversation . . .

Imagine that the year is 2030, and a planet has been discovered around a star 100 light years away. Measurements made by a space telescope show that the planet has a similar composition to Earth's. A radio signal is sent to the planet, taking 100 years to reach it. Any reply will take at least 200 years to arrive back at Earth.

The year is 2230. Excitement builds as a reply is awaited to the signal sent 200 years ago. One of the astronomers involved in the search is the great great great grand-daughter of one of the team that originally sent the message back in 2030.

25 July, 2230. A reply is received, showing that there is an alien civilisation on the planet, and it understood our message. The reply is quickly deciphered, and seems to show that the alien creatures are friendly. A response is put together on Earth, and quickly transmitted to the other civilisation.

It is decided to send a team of astronauts to the aliens' planet. The journey will take over 500 years to complete. The spacecraft is like a spaceship Earth, and several generations will live and die on the journey to the other planet. The people who reach the planet will be the distant descendants of the astronauts who set out from Earth.

The year is 2430. Excitement builds as a reply is awaited to the signal sent 200 years ago. This time, no signal is received. The astronomers keep the listening programme running for another 50 years, and then abandon the project.
If the people who travelled to the planet ever reach their destination, no one knows what they will find.

So a cosmic conversation would be incredibly slow, with hundreds or thousands of years between messages. Perhaps aliens live for thousands of years so that it wouldn't matter to them, but to humans on Earth it would certainly be very frustrating. It would be much better if we could meet aliens. But travelling to their planets would take even longer – travel through space cannot be faster than the speed of light, which is the speed at which radio signals travel.

INTERSTELLAR
CALLS

SPACETIME

So much space and so little time! But there may be a way around this problem. We might be able to manipulate space and time, to make the journey quicker. To understand how, we have to be physicists and consider what space and time really are. The most famous physicist, Albert Einstein, did just that in his theories of relativity. He visualised space and time as an inter-woven 'fabric' called spacetime. We don't have space or time in this book to explain spacetime properly*, but for now, you can picture spacetime as a stretched rubber sheet.

---

* See *What's the Big Idea? Time and the Universe* for more about spacetime.

You have probably heard of black holes. Some physicists have suggested that they could be the entrances to tunnels that lead to a different place and time. These tunnels are often called wormholes, and it is suggested that they connect two black holes in different parts of spacetime.

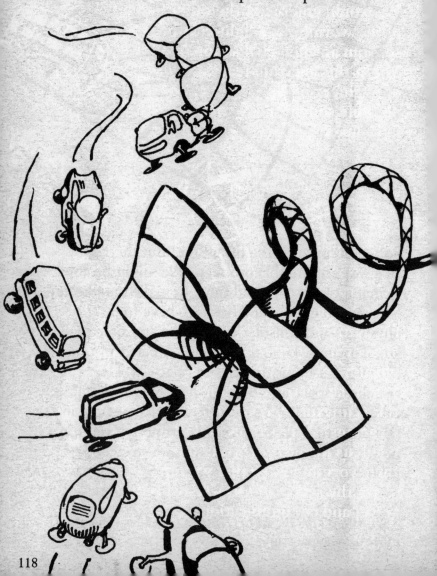

Could wormholes provide us with a fast-track to outer space? Clever use of these cosmic motorways could cut the journey time to the nearest star from, say, 5,000 years to perhaps a year. Perhaps we could build an artificial black hole nearby, and use it to travel. We would emerge at the other end of the wormhole, a light year or so from an alien civilisation. Might this amazing feat of engineering be possible some time in the next century?

Perhaps alien civilisations are already using wormholes to visit Earth (that would explain those unexplained UFO sightings). Maybe they will teach us how to construct our own wormholes, so that we can share the secret of ultra-fast space travel and communication.

ALIEN LIFE
FACT OR FICTION ?

Imagine if you were a member of the jury in
a court case about alien life. What would
you decide?

MEMBERS OF THE JURY, YOUR TASK IS TO CONSIDER
WHETHER ALIEN LIFE EXISTS, BASED ON THE
EVIDENCE BEFORE YOU. WE HAVE SEEN THAT
IT IS UNLIKELY THAT EARTH IS THE ONLY
PLANET IN THE ENTIRE UNIVERSE WHERE
CONDITIONS ARE JUST RIGHT FOR LIFE TO
ARISE. HOWEVER, IF THERE IS LIFE OUT
THERE, WHY HAVE WE FOUND NO DEFINITE
EVIDENCE OF IT ?

WHEN MAKING YOUR JUDGEMENT, YOU MUST REMEMBER THE CONVINCING EVIDENCE OF SIGHTINGS OF UFOs FROM THROUGHOUT HISTORY AND FROM ACROSS THE WORLD. IS THIS ENOUGH TO MAKE YOU CERTAIN OF THE EXISTENCE OF ALIEN LIFE? REMEMBER THAT NOT ONE OF THE SIGHTINGS HAS BEEN SHOWN TO BE INDISPUTABLE. WE HAVE HEARD THAT TRAVEL FROM ONE CIVILISATION TO ANOTHER ACROSS SPACE WOULD TAKE A VERY LONG TIME, BUT WE HAVE ALSO HEARD THAT INTELLIGENT EXTRATERRESTRIALS COULD USE WORMHOLES THROUGH SPACETIME TO REACH EARTH QUICKLY. HOWEVER, FOR NOW WORMHOLES REMAIN IN THE REALM OF SCIENCE FICTION.

MEMBERS OF THE JURY, WHAT IS YOUR VERDICT?

If a communication is received from an alien civilisation, or better still, if we are visited by members of an alien race, will it change our lives?

- WOULD THERE BE CHAOS AND UNCERTAINTY ABOUT WHAT IT ALL MEANS?

- WOULD SOME PEOPLE BELIEVE THE WHOLE THING TO BE AN ELABORATE HOAX?

- WOULD WE HAVE A GREAT DEAL TO LEARN FROM INTELLIGENT EXTRATERRESTRIALS?

- WOULD OUR SCIENTIFIC THEORIES AND THEREFORE OUR UNDERSTANDING OF THE WORLD AROUND US HAVE TO BE UPDATED OR CHANGED?

- WOULD WE ADOPT THE ALIENS' TECHNOLOGY, LEARNING HOW TO MAKE NEW MATERIALS, CURE ALL ILLNESSES AND TRAVEL IN TIME FOR EXAMPLE?

- WOULD IT UNITE OUR WORLD?

- WOULD THE WORLD'S RELIGIONS NEED TO ADJUST TO THE NEW INFORMATION?

Whether we discover alien life or not, it is certainly worth thinking about — it's a very big idea indeed.

Finding out more

Internet resources

SETI Institute
A must for anyone interested in the search for alien life.
http://www.seti-inst.edu/
SETI Institute
2035 Landings Drive
Mountain View, CA
94043 USA
Tel: 00 1 (650) 961-6633

SETIQuest®
This American magazine is available over the Internet or by post. It is up-to-date, but rather expensive. You can try out a free sample issue at:
http://www.setiquest.com/nfreeis.htm
Or you can find out more by contacting:
Helmers Publishing, Inc.
174 Concord Street
Peterborough, NH 03458-0874
Tel: 00 1 (603) 924 9631

Astrobiology Web
An excellent and easy to use source of information about alien life, presented by Reston Communications®.
http://www.reston.com/astro/seti.html

CNI News
This is an e-magazine that has up-to-date information on 'contact with non-human intelligence' (CNI). You can get two free issues by visiting the website below, but after that you have to pay.
http://www.cninews.com/
2100 W. Drake Rd.
#277 Fort Collins, CO
80526 USA.

Books

Is Anyone Out There? The Scientific Search for Extraterrestrial Intelligence
Frank Drake and Dava Sobel.
Published by Delacorte Press, 1992.
Co-written by Frank Drake himself.

Murmurs of Earth: The Voyager Interstellar Record
Sagan, Sagan, Drake, Druyan, Ferris, Lomberg.
Published by Warner New Media, 1992.
Previously issued as a book, this boxed set CD-ROM contains the music, sounds and images contained on the two Voyager spacecraft.

U.F.O. Evaluating the Evidence
Bill Yenne
Published by Grange Books, 1997.
A good read that is well-researched.

ETs and UFOs: Are They Real?
Larry Kettelkamp
Published by William Morrow & Company, 1996.

Life on Mars
David Getz, Peter McCarty (Illustrator)
Published by Henry Holt & Company, Inc. 1997.

The Unexplained Series: UFOs and Aliens
Colin Wilson
Published by Dorling Kindersley, 1997.

Fire in the Sky: The Walton Experience
Travis Walton
Published by Shooting Star, 1996.

Glossary

alien
Describing anything that does not originate from Earth.

galaxy
A huge group of thousands or millions of stars. Our star, the Sun, is in a galaxy that we call the Milky Way.

gravitational pull
The force that keeps you on the ground, also known as gravity. Gravitational pull between the Sun and the Earth stops the Earth moving off into space in a straight line: gravity keeps the Earth in orbit.

life
Well, what is it? The dictionary describes life in many ways, but one of the best is 'a state characterized by capacity for metabolism, growth, reaction to stimuli, and reproduction'.

organic molecules
Any molecules that are involved in life processes, in particular DNA and proteins. All known organic molecules are based on the element carbon.

radio signals / radio waves
Electromagnetic radiation, like light and X-rays but with a longer wavelength. Radio waves pass across the vast distances of space, and so may be used by alien civilisations to send messages.

SETI
The 'search for extraterrestrial intelligence', which involves hunting the sky for signals from alien civilisations.

Solar System
The Sun, nine planets (including Earth) and their moons, and millions of comets, asteroids and other objects that orbit the Sun.

space probe
A robot spacecraft that explores our Moon, other planets and their moons, or other objects in space.

star
A huge ball of hot gas in space, that gives off light. All stars, except the Sun, are so far away that they appear as dim points of light in our night sky.

UFO
Abbreviation for 'unidentified flying object'.

INDEX

WHAT'S THE BIG IDEA?

Have you read them all?

0 304 722630	Alien Life	£3.99	☐
0 304 667206	Animal Rights	£3.99	☐
0 304 67847X	The Environment	£3.99	☐
0 304 724056	Food*	£3.99	☐
0 304 708778	Genetics	£3.99	☐
0 304 722916	The Media*	£3.99	☐
0 304 655887	The Mind	£3.99	☐
0 304 693398	Nuclear Power	£3.99	☐
0 304 714824	The Paranormal*	£3.99	☐
0 304 667192	Religion	£3.99	☐
0 304 655909	Time and the Universe	£3.99	☐
0 304 655917	Virtual Reality	£3.99	☐
0 304 655895	Women's Rights	£3.99	☐

* coming soon

Turn the page to find out how to order these books.

ORDER FORM

Books in this series are available at your local bookshop, or can be ordered direct from the publisher. A complete list of titles is given on the previous page. Just tick the title you would like and complete the details below. Prices and availability are subject to change without prior notice.

Please enclose a cheque or postal order made payable to Bookpoint Ltd, and send to: Hodder Children's Books, Cash Sales Dept, Bookpoint, 39 Milton Park, Abingdon, Oxon OX14 4TD.
Email address: orders@bookpoint.co.uk.

If you would prefer to pay by credit card, our call centre team would be delighted to take your order by telephone. Our direct line is 01235 400414 (lines open 9.00 am – 6.00 pm, Monday to Saturday; 24 hour message answering service). Alternatively you can send a fax on 01235 400454.

Title .... First name .... Surname ....

Address ....

....

....

Daytime tel .... Postcode ....

If you would prefer to post a credit card order, please complete the following.

Please debit my Visa/Access/Diners Card/American Express (delete as applicable) card number:

Signature .... Expiry Date ....

If you would NOT like to receive further information on our products, please tick ☐ .